W9-CUB-761

CONSUMER GUIDE®

QUICK FIXES

Home Organization &
Storage

pil Publications International, Ltd.

Mary Wynn Ryan is the author of numerous interior design books, including *The Ultimate Kitchen, Cottage Style, Urban Style, Decorating Kids' Rooms*, and *Garden Style*. She has written about home furnishings and interior design for various magazines and served as Midwest editor of *Design Times* magazine. Ryan was also the director of consumer and trade marketing for the Chicago Merchandise Mart's residential design center. She is president of Winning Ways Marketing, an editorial and marketing consulting firm that specializes in home design and decorating.

Louis Weber, CEO
Publications International, Ltd.
7373 North Cicero Avenue
Lincolnwood, Illinois 60712

ISBN-13: 978-1-4127-8291-3
ISBN-10: 1-4127-8291-0

Manufactured in U.S.A.

8 7 6 5 4 3 2 1

CONTENTS

THE TIME OF YOUR LIFE

We all have the same 24 hours a day; no more, no less. How many hours do you lose because you can't find crucial paperwork, such as bills, receipts, and kids' permission slips? Let's face it: When we're disorganized, even for good reasons, we put our money, our credibility, and our peace of mind at risk. When our whole house is a giant junk drawer, life is much harder than it has to be.

Are you way too busy to get organized? Start somewhere: Invest 15 minutes or a half hour a day and you'll save twice that in aggravated hunting and foraging. Organization is liberation. We'll show you how to get there and save your precious time for the important things.

Hectic schedules can't always be avoided, but they don't have to result in chaos. We'll show you how to organize your family's time, your shopping trips, your home in general, and those especially tricky spaces—the closet and home office—where chaos often takes over.

You *can* get organized a little at a time, so don't sabotage yourself by saying you'd do it "if you had more time." You *will* have more time—as soon as you take charge. You'll see!

CHAPTER ONE

HOW TO KEEP TRACK WITH LISTS, PLANNERS, AND CALENDARS

Everyone is so busy these days, even the kids. You can't keep everything in your head, so don't even try. Use lists, calendars, and planners to record dates and deadlines as they show up in your life, and save your brain for more creative problem solving.

- Create a central place near the phone to keep a handle on family dates and deadlines. Use a large calendar that has the biggest squares you can find so you can fit everyone's events in each square. Choose one that has a blank area not allocated to a date so that you can make a quick note of something important where it won't get lost. Pick a

Sunday	Monday	Tuesday	Wednesday	Thursday	Friday	Saturday
		1	2	3	4	5
6	7	8	9	10	11	12
13	14	15	16	17	18	19
0	21	22	23	24	25	
28	29					

calendar that's not too fussy and that lets you make notes and see what's going on even when you're in a rush. Shop office supply catalogs and stores for the calendar that works for you.

- Keep written communications with deadline-sensitive information in an accordion-style folder next to the calendar. As soon as the item comes into the house, write the basics on the calendar. If you get really rushed and can't record the item right away, stash it in the folder and record it on the calendar later that day. If you prefer, get a calendar with a built-in shallow pocket at the bottom; it holds less, so you won't be tempted to let material pile up. **Important:** Go through the accordion folder or pocket at least twice a week—say, on Wednesday and Saturday—to be sure you have transferred key dates to the master calendar.

- Use the calendar to see the big picture, and use lists to get things done. Make a list each week, perhaps on Saturday or Sunday morning, of all the family's to-do items you know about at the time. Then on Tuesday and again on Thursday, take 10 minutes with the whole family to go over the list so everyone knows what's up. If John needs new crayons to do a social studies poster or Sara has promised to babysit, any time (or chauffeuring!) conflicts can be addressed before they become a crisis.

- Create a weekly "Family Chores List," and have family members sign up for chores. This gives everyone some say in what they're going to do, and the whole family can share the responsibility of getting things done. (When kids squabble over who gets the "easy" chore, tell them the jobs will switch next week.) Remind your child to put today's chores on his or her daily list (see next tip).

- Help each family member make a short daily list every night, taking items from the weekly list and calendar plus any last-minute updates. Kids old enough to read appreciate the freedom (and the reduced nagging) a list gives them. In addition to family chores, add everyday activities such as "take shower" and "do homework" to the list, and see if it cuts down on verbal reminders.

- Use a yearly planner to record internal deadline dates on the road to long-term goals, such as buying a house or planning vacations. Transfer these dates to the family calendar.

Keeping updated lists is a new habit, so give yourself a month or two to make it part of your natural routine. Most people, even kids, find checking off items gives a sense of accomplishment, as well as reminding them of what they still need to do. Kids are expected to use assignment notebooks in school, so it may be easier than you think.

You and the kids will discover that when things don't fall through the cracks, excuses don't have to be made, and everyone's life is more comfortable.

CHAPTER TWO

HOW TO PRIORITIZE AND GET THINGS DONE

Everyone's energy ebbs and flows, and you can get a surprisingly great amount of work done in less time if you go with the flow. First, maximize your energy by getting enough sleep at night (and catnap if you can't), eat protein and good carbohydrates (not delicious-but-empty sugary carbs) to maintain your blood sugar level, and exercise at least 20 minutes every day. Beyond that, make the most of whatever energy you have by working smart.

- Decide on the time of day when your energy level is highest to do your toughest chore. You'll find you can get through it much more easily. If you're a morning person, tackle the hard stuff first and wind down the day with a chore you find easier. If you hit your stride later on, ease into your day with the less-demanding chores and work up to the harder ones. Many people experience a low energy level at about 3:00 P.M. If this is you, plan to do your no-brainer jobs then, but take a quick walk or grab a cup of joe first so you don't get caught napping.

- If you don't do first things first, make sure you get to the essential projects *sometime* during the day. Start early enough to finish what you start. Don't let the obvious, the handy, and the urgent tasks crowd out the actually important ones!

- If you have trouble getting started in the morning, do as much as you can the night before. Lay out your clothes, measure the coffee, and pack lunches before you go to bed. Have the kids lay out their clothes and pack up permission slips and projects, and you'll all have a much less stressful morning.

- With a huge project, begin at the end: Determine the final deadline you need to meet in order to achieve your goal, and work back from there. Set internal deadlines to make sure you stay on track throughout the project. Most projects have internal deadlines triggered by outside influences: a college tuition due date, a time frame for booking an airline ticket, etc. If yours doesn't, set deadlines at the one-quarter, halfway, and three-quarter points in time. It's much easier to catch up when you're only a little behind schedule. Kids also can use this approach to study for a major exam on which a lot of material is covered or to get a major homework presentation done on time without "cramming."

- Set realistic goals. Don't try to do too much in one day or even one year. If you find yourself constantly behind schedule, keep a notepad with you and write down everything you do for a few days. Then look at the list objectively to determine whether you've attempted to do too much in too short a time. Allocate more time to certain stages of the work by extending the deadline if you can. If it's an outside deadline you can't control, look at your list to see what nonessentials can be dropped or done with shortcuts. You don't have to say "yes" to every request or do everything "from scratch" to get the benefit.

- Accept that certain projects, such as home remodeling, always take longer—sometimes significantly longer—than anyone expects. The more unknowns (such as, what's behind that old wall?) in a project, the more possible delays. Interior deadlines can help somewhat, but don't plan a major home renovation six months before a home wedding. For any type of project, try to build in extra time in case the unexpected happens. And be sure to build in regular times for a little family bonding, fun, and relaxation. You'll be more efficient afterward!

- Get the family involved in day-to-day chores. Even young children can set the table or put newspapers in the recycling bin. If school activities and homework prevent older children from taking on weekday chores, get them involved for a couple of hours on the weekends—in half-hour blocks, of course. Give them a list to work from, with breaks in between.

HOW TO SHOP EFFICIENTLY

Unless your budget is unlimited or you're out for some "retail therapy," you probably want your shopping expeditions to be efficient. These days, few of us have the funds to come home with meaningless purchases, and none of us has the time to come home empty-handed because we didn't plan or organize well. Follow these tips for a more successful shopping experience.

Shopping for Groceries

Food isn't cheap, and it's something you can't defer purchasing, so it pays to shop smartly. Organize your shopping so you can eat better for less.

- Create menus for the week before you go shopping and make a list that includes everything you'll need to make the meals on your menus. Check your cupboards for staples and spices before you shop to avoid buying doubles (and to be sure you have what you think you have).

- Pin menus for the week on a bulletin board in the kitchen. If you're using recipes from a cookbook, list the recipe titles and cookbook page references. That way, the first person home can start dinner.

- It's very annoying to be halfway through fixing a recipe before discovering you're all out of eggs, milk, or whatever is needed to finish the job, because you didn't know somebody used it all up. Post a shopping list in the kitchen and establish a rule that whoever uses the last of an item immediately puts it on the list. This method goes a long way toward avoiding last-minute shopping trips for missing items.

- Don't feel sheepish about faithfully using coupons. Studies show better educated, more affluent consumers actually make more use of coupons than others do. Small savings add up!

- If you shop regularly at the same store, write your shopping list in the same order as the food is stocked in the store aisles.

- Be aware that basic, must-have foods such as milk and bread are usually stocked around the perimeter of the store so you have to traverse the whole place to get to them. Novelty snack foods and other impulse items are displayed near the entrance and at the end of store aisles, where they're easy to see. Shop from your list and don't get distracted.

- Go grocery shopping when it's least crowded—perhaps in the early morning or late evening.

- Never shop on an empty stomach!

- Manufacturers use coupons to entice you to try items you haven't purchased before. Look at sale coupons in the newspaper to see if any of your usual purchases are on sale, but don't buy items you wouldn't ordinarily buy just because they're on sale—unless you'd really like to try them, of course.

- Store coupons in a small accordion file with labels for different types of food, such as Meat, Pasta, Fruit, etc. Regularly check the newspaper and online for coupons, and add sale items to your shopping list. Take your file with you to the store to make sure you take advantage of every sale you can. Take 15 minutes every week or two to weed out obsolete coupons, as most store scanners will reject them.

- Keep a good supply of staple foods on hand and make sure you can prepare at least one or two meals completely from canned and packaged items, such as pasta and spaghetti sauce with mushrooms or meat or tuna noodle casserole. Keep bottled juice, canned soups, peanut butter, crackers, and the like on hand for a good stopgap snack or light meal.

- If you shop for such commodities as paper towels in bulk at a big-box discount store, plan where you'll store these items ahead of time. Provided they're kept clean and dry, nonfood items like these can be stored in the basement or even the garage.

- Follow the same approach for trips to the drugstore as you're using for grocery shopping. Have family members put personal care items on a list as soon as they notice an item is running low to avoid the trauma of running out of toothpaste or other toiletries. Check for drugstore coupons in the newspaper too, and keep them in your grocery accordion file or in a separate one.

- Take advantage of sales on recipe items you use a lot: Cook a double batch and freeze half for the inevitable rush day when you don't have time to shop but need to get a meal on the table—fast. Be sure to store meals in freezer-safe packaging to avoid thawing or freezer burn.

Shopping for Clothing

Clothing offers plenty of opportunities for saving money and just as many opportunities to squander it. Organize your clothing shopping, and you'll be able to take advantage of great deals without breaking the bank.

- Avoid the disappointment of finding out an outfit is just not right when you get it home. When you go shopping for a particular item of clothing, wear the kind of underwear and accessories that you would wear with it. If you're shopping for a jacket, wear a shirt and tie; if you're shopping for a party dress, wear the right lingerie and shoes. Take the guesswork out of it and minimize time-wasting returns or getting stuck with a final sale item that doesn't work for you.

- Kids grow fast, so it's easier than you think to lose track of what size they are. That's inconvenient when you're standing in front of a great item on markdown but you don't know if it will fit. Have your kids try on everything for the upcoming season twice a year—in the early spring and early fall—so you can start replacing items they've outgrown as you see sales. (Some kids will enjoy this process and others won't, so do what you can to make it palatable. You may need to break up the process into two or three sessions.) Immediately take outgrown items out of their drawers and closets and pass them down to a sibling or along to another family.

- Keep an updated index card in your wallet with the sizes and measurements of all your family members. You'll be prepared to take advantage of an unexpected bargain and avoid returning items that don't fit.

- If you want to match a color perfectly, take the item (or a small fabric scrap snipped from a hem) with you. Your eye may not see color as accurately as you think, and store lighting is different than home lighting, which also affects how color looks. Realistically, unless you are shopping from the same season as the item you're matching, you may have difficulty getting a true match. Manufacturers change colors slightly to spur sales, and last year's burgundy may not be the same as this year's. A better strategy is to buy an item in a coordinating, not matching, color.

- Avoid the "nothing to wear" syndrome by building your wardrobe around a few favorite colors and go-with-everything neutrals. Even kids can benefit from this approach, as most have one or two favorite colors, and family members will appreciate knowing what colors are preferred for gifts. Your outfits will look good, it will be easy to pull them together, and you'll avoid the mismatched look and wasted money of impulse purchases.

- Do as the better clothing stores do: Organize your closet by clothing type (skirts, blouses, etc.) and then by color. When everything goes with everything, getting dressed in a hurry will be easy.

- If you're starting a new lifestyle (going back to work, enjoying retirement), you may need to buy more than usual in a season. Buy the best basics you can afford in versatile neutrals and your two or three selected colors, and punch up the look with accessories that include both neutrals or your colors and the latest fashion hues.

- Shop for your actual lifestyle. Some jobs actually require lots of dressy clothes or very casual clothes, but most don't. Business casual works in many situations, and business style works for most of the rest. Organize your closet for easiest access to what you wear most.

- Make a list of your major clothing items by season. You may find you're missing some special pieces, such as pastel wools for chilly springs, dark cottons for sultry autumns, a black raincoat that can double as an evening coat, etc. If you know what you're missing, you can shop sales for these items instead of ending up with novelty pieces that don't really solve wardrobe needs.

- In today's competitive retail climate, clothing goes on sale year-round, but you can still find extra bargains at certain times. For example, new bathing suits come out in January for the resort season, but they go on sale in June in plenty of time for the swimming season. Deepest discounts appear in August, and by September, it may be difficult to find a suit until after Christmas. Winter coats and dressy items go on sale after Christmas, and fall apparel is marked down. If you don't need to have the very latest look and you like classic styles, you can fill in wardrobe gaps with end-of-season deals in fine quality apparel.

CHAPTER THREE

HOW TO ORGANIZE HOUSEHOLD PAPERWORK

Chasing paper wastes time and energy. And when bills aren't paid or permission slips aren't turned in, the price for disorganization is penalty payments, missed field trips, and stress. If your idea of organizing your papers is to stack them on the dining room table, invest an hour in setting up a system that will do some work for *you*.

• Designate one or two drawers in your home as the place to file important papers. If possible, use a wood two-drawer file cabinet that can double as an end table. They are available in rustic Mission, 18th-century traditional, and modern styles to blend with your décor. For more storage space, buy two as matching end tables or nightstands. Keep it (or them) conveniently located so you can immediately stash paperwork rather than leaving important papers all over the house.

• Use file folders in assorted colors from the office supply store. Colored folders make filing easier and quicker (it's easier to see colors than to read labels). Maybe just as important, colored folders make filing feel less like work, whether you designate a color for each family member and category or just use them randomly. Use the categories in "How to Set Up Your Filing System" on page 19 to organize your file folders.

- Set up an individual folder for each family member so you can conveniently stash clippings, awards, cards, and save-worthy homework projects for each person.

- File unpaid bills in a "To Be Paid" folder (a red folder may help) where you'll see them but others won't. Pay bills at least twice a month so you won't incur late fees.

- File paid bills in separate folders or large envelopes labeled by month and year so you can stash them elsewhere at year's end without worry.

- Use a "Miscellaneous" file for items that don't easily fit into a category, but be sure to go through this file once a month before it fills up. When you accumulate a number of items on the same topic, create a new category file for them. Unneeded items will be easily recognizable.

- Use a "To Be Filed" file for when you're really rushed, but make a commitment to file these items in their proper folders once a week. It's important to at least put all incoming paperwork into one central location, out of sight but not out of mind.

- Put a check from your checkbook in your wallet in case you need one when you don't have your checkbook. Record the check number in your check register and note in pencil that it's your emergency check so you won't wonder what you did with it later. When you use the check, go back and record the amount and payee.

- Make use of all those printed address labels you get from charities. Use them to quickly fill in coupons and rebate forms; label books, tools, and other items you lend to neighbors; label dishes you take to potluck suppers; and identify items you leave to be fixed at repair shops.

- If you're the article-clipping type, keep an attractive pocket folder near your chair to corral the sheets you tear out. If you're really clip-happy, make it an accordion file and label each pocket with a main topic or theme on which you like to collect articles.

- If you have school-age children, keep a special clipboard or basket near the door for all those permission slips and other school documents that are easily lost. It's hard enough to get kids to deliver these papers to you, but at least once you've got your hands on them you'll know where they are and when they have to be processed. Commit to going through this pile twice a week to catch any deadline-sensitive materials, and transfer these dates to the family calendar. You don't want to miss school picture day!

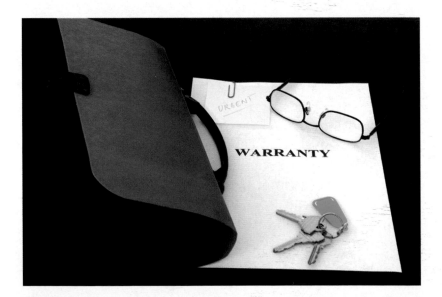

How to Set Up Your Filing System

WHAT TO FILE AT HOME:
- **Banking**—check registers, extra checks, passbooks, canceled checks
- **Car**—titles, insurance policies, maintenance records, payments
- **Credit cards**—list of all credit cards with numbers, statements
- **Guarantees and warranties** (include instruction pamphlets)
- **House records**—homeowners insurance policy and mortgage papers; home improvement receipts; lease and renters insurance policy, if renting
- **Investment records**—mutual fund and broker statements
- **Life insurance policies**
- **Medical records**—immunizations, insurance forms, insurance payments, prescriptions
- **Tax records**—copies of tax records for previous years, receipts for deductible expenses you plan to claim on next year's return, real estate tax bills
- **Copy of will** (keep other copy at your attorney's office)

WHAT TO STORE IN THE BANK DEPOSIT BOX:
- **Personal papers**—birth certificates, marriage license, passports, military service records, divorce decrees
- **House deed and title**
- **Financial holdings**—savings bonds, bank certificates of deposit, stock certificates
- **List of valuables** (include room-by-room videotape of home, if possible)

- If your kids are on sports teams or in another activity that generates deadlines, schedules, and paperwork, keep these materials in the kids' basket (see previous tip). Go through this twice a week and transfer key dates to the calendar.

- Put a decorative box or basket near your front door for keys and outbound mail. That way, you'll always know where your keys are, and when you grab your keys, you'll remember to take out the mail.

- Instead of using an address book, try using a more flexible system of index cards stored in a file box. Along with names, addresses, and phone numbers, you'll have room to keep track of birthdays, anniversaries, clothing sizes, and even presents you've given in recent years. If someone moves, substitute an updated card.

- If you collect business cards, consider a ring-binder notebook with sleeves sized to hold business cards. Or just pop them into your address file box (see previous tip).

- Keep instruction booklets that come with appliances all in one box, such as the kind used to store photos. Or, if you don't usually refer to instructions once you're set up, stash them in the "Warranties" folder (see "How to Set Up Your Filing System" on page 19).

- Review your filing system monthly and toss out items you no longer need, such as warranties on discarded appliances.

- Make filing less tedious by filing while watching TV. File during the commercials, and you'll be done before you know it.

CHAPTER FOUR

TOP MANAGEMENT FOR YOUR HOME OFFICE

Home offices just keep on growing in importance. Whether you need a home office for telecommuting, for your entrepreneurial business, or just as command central on the home front, it's worth setting up right.

PLANNING AND FURNISHING YOUR HOME OFFICE

If you're running a home-based business, you'll obviously need more space and equipment than if you're just looking for a place to file personal papers and pay household bills. Home office areas tend to swell and take over whatever room they're in, so it's better not to start using the dining room table!

To get just what you need, think about all the people who'll use your home office and figure carefully all the things they'll need to do there. Then choose from the following tips to put together a cost-effective home office that looks good and works as hard as you do.

SPACE PLANNING

- Measure twice, shop once. Before you head out to buy furniture and equipment for your home office, draw up a floor plan with accurate measurements. This is especially important if your space is scant, because conventional office furniture tends to be bulky.

Measure the area or room, and draw the space on graph paper to scale; be sure to draw in windows and doors. Then play with various design plans to fit.

- Figure out how many phone lines and grounded electrical outlets you'll need for computers and other office equipment. If you can, situate your new furniture where you can take advantage of existing outlets, but don't sacrifice a workable plan for existing outlets. Plan for more than you think you'll need, and save money by doing the whole job at once when you hire the electrician. Simpler yet, consider wireless Internet access and a cordless phone anchored in another room.

- Make a rough list of the paperwork and other items your office storage needs to handle: personal files, sales records, drawing materials, outstanding orders, contracts, price lists, correspondence, etc. In each case, write down a brief description and quantity, then note how frequently you'll need to access it. Plan to keep current documents within easy reach, less active records in a nearby area, and permanent, seldom-used records in a more remote location.

- Allow at least three feet in front of a set of shelves for easy access.

- Give yourself at least three feet between your task chair and a wall or another piece of furniture so you can get in and out easily.

- Allow at least two feet between two pieces of furniture or a piece of furniture and a wall for a comfortable walkway. This doesn't include space for drawers or cabinets to open, so allow extra room for those functions.

- If your desk is more than 30 inches deep, use the wall next to the desk for a bulletin board. If your desk is less than 30 inches deep, you can use the wall opposite the desk.

- If you need to see clients, even casually, set up your office where you can maintain a little quiet and order; ideally in a guest or spare room.

- If you can avoid it, don't put a full office setup in your master bedroom; it's too hard to turn off work mode at night. If space is tight and you just need a spot to pay the bills, however, a lightly scaled, pretty desk and occasional chair in the bedroom may be fine.

- If your office is in a guest bedroom or another dual-function space, look for dual-function furniture such as a daybed, a sofa bed (provided you have the floor space to pull it out), and lots of wall units for open and closed storage. Set things up so a work surface is near enough to the daybed to function as a nightstand, and make sure reading light over the daybed is adequate too.

STORAGE

- If you're very short on floor space, mount shelves on a wall above desk height to store files in handsome, lightweight rattan boxes, and station a folding table beneath it.

- If you buy printer paper and other supplies in bulk, plan for safe storage. The ideal is a dedicated office supply closet, but if you can't manage that, stash supplies in low built-in cupboards, in a steamer trunk/coffee table, or elsewhere in your space. Paper and many other supplies are sensitive to temperature and moisture, so store them with care to preserve your bulk purchase investment.

- Choose freestanding shelving units for the most flexible, budget-friendly storage option, but remember to factor in the cost of baskets or boxes to keep shelf storage neat and contents out of sight. Don't skimp on shelf quality; papers and books are heavy and need strong, sturdy boards and plenty of support.

• Hang wall-mounted magazine racks above or next to the desk to keep current paperwork and reference materials in sight without taking up desk space.

• For ultimate flexibility, put storage on casters. Artists' tabourets, rolling files, and other ingenious solutions let you wheel storage into a temporary workspace and out again for everyday use of the room. If you opt for wireless Internet access and a cell phone, you can even put your desk on wheels.

• Spray paint two-drawer file cabinets to match room schemes if you'd like a more colorful look than what's commonly available. Metal file cabinets have sharp corners, so confine these to rooms and areas where kids won't be tempted to roughhouse.

• Whether you use multiple colored boxes, wicker baskets, or other storage bins, make sure you label their contents. Opaque storage is neat, but you don't want to waste time looking for what you need. Hang labels from ribbons or glue them on; use a method you can easily replace or cover over.

• Consider stock kitchen cabinetry for home office storage. Deep drawers designed for pots and pans can hold files, and the mix of drawers and cabinets lets you stash lots of office gear out of sight. Some kitchen cabinet lines include a desk, which makes it even easier.

- Put an office armoire to work in virtually any room. They're prewired for electronics and feature a drop-down work surface that goes undercover when the armoire doors are shut. If you're stuck with an older TV armoire and don't need it for your HD flat screen, see if you can use it for office storage. The partitions may not be exactly what you want, but these units can hold a lot of office supplies behind closed doors.

- Convert an ordinary chest of drawers into a lateral file cabinet by fitting drawer interiors with inserts or dividers. To store file folders upright, you'll need a chest with drawers at least ten inches deep. Letter-size file folders are just under 12 inches wide, so a chest that's 24, 36, or 48 inches wide is most efficient. If your chest is an odd width, fill in the gap next to folders with a narrow box for office supplies.

- For home office or home entertainment, store wires by bundling them into flexible hollow tubes. Be sure to identify the equipment each wire goes to by means of a small hangtag label on each wire before you bundle them.

Tax Considerations

If you are using your home office for business, many expenses can be tax deductible. However, your home office must be used *exclusively* and *regularly* as a *principal* place of business or no tax deductions are allowed. If your home office meets this all-important test, some available tax deductions include: expense for a second phone line; depreciation of the portion of your home that constitutes the office; a percentage of expenses such as utility bills; and purchase of business-related equipment. Be aware, however, that deductions can be made only against income generated by a home business, not against income generated in other employment, and that a home office cannot generate a tax loss. Be sure to consult your tax accountant before making major decisions that may impact your home-office tax status.

- In a family room with both media room and home office components, use built-ins along two walls—one for the home office and the other for home entertainment electronics. Position the desk so you can see the TV if you like during rote projects that don't demand a lot of mental attention.

- Make sure you provide room for file cabinet drawers to open all the way. Conventional file cabinets are often deeper than a desk, and with drawers extended, they'll need even more floor space. Allow at least three feet in front of a filing cabinet so that you can open the drawers easily. Lateral files are wider but less deep, so measure your space and select the units that work for you.

- If your home office includes space for crafts, consider nontraditional storage for all those little odds and ends. A lingerie chest, an artist's tabouret, or other storage pieces with multiple small drawers or trays make it easy to stash small items such as buttons, stamps, and ribbon.

- Vertical files make it easy to see a lot of project folders at once, without having to handle them. Use one or more for current projects and keep them on your desktop for easy access.

- Store expensive equipment behind closed doors if your home office is visible from the street, and store important records, irreplaceable work, and confidential files in locking fireproof cabinets.

- Just as with other household storage, remember rule No. 1: Store items you use often nearby and items you use seldom in more remote locations. If your work surface is getting smaller by the day, it's time to move some of the stuff on top of it to drawers or other storage.

OFFICE FURNITURE

- In a family room home office, buy an angled desk or create an L- or U-shape desk for maximum efficiency. Create a U-shape or L-shape desk by combining a conventional desk with a credenza, file cabinets, worktables, or a drop-leaf table. Position the extra work surface perpendicular to your desk or main work surface for an L-shape setup, and add a third wing for a U-shape plan. The goal is to keep everything you use daily easily within arm's reach so you don't have to get up unless you want to stretch your legs.

- On a shared worktable, plan for about 30 inches of space for each person.

- Provide a file drawer for each person to make it easy to safely stash projects out of sight.

- Invest in a cabinet with wide, flat file drawers, like the kind architects use, if you or the kids generate large paper projects such as maps or posters.

• If your spouse needs at-home workspace too, consider a classic partner desk (with kneeholes on opposite sides and a deep enough worktop for two) that may be ideal for the pair of you.

• If you're designing a new kitchen, plan on an efficient desk nook with shelves overhead for cookbooks and file drawers beneath for financial and personal files. Station the big family calendar here, along with the phone. If there's a spare wall nearby, paint it with magnetic paint and finish with a coat or two of your regular wall paint. You'll have plenty of room to hang schedules, invitations, and the like. Keep things neat and functional by purchasing a set of matching magnets, and prune out the display every week.

• If you simply need space to pay bills and write notes, select a handsome secretary. This elegant, traditional desk with drawers below and display shelves above is a pretty addition to the bedroom. Just be sure you can fit file folders into the drawers, or add a traditionally styled wood two-drawer file as a nightstand.

- For a nostalgic country look, consider a rolltop desk. The top rolls down to conceal paper clutter—ideal if your home office area is in the family room or another public space. Cubbyholes above the work surface make it easy to store office supplies. Matching wood file cabinets complete the plan.

- For an elegant traditional room, choose a drop-front desk (also referred to as a "drop-lid" desk). Like the rolltop, the drop-front desk hides home office clutter in style and includes a variety of cubbyholes for small office supply storage. Just make sure you allow enough room in front for the drop leaf to come down. For occasional use, you could even place a drop-front desk in a wide hallway and pull up a side chair when needed.

- Shop nontraditional sources for office furniture to meet your needs. Check out office supply stores, furniture stores, big-box stores such as IKEA, and Internet retailers for a wealth of options in a range of styles and prices. Don't overlook used office furniture stores; you may find great bargains on pieces engineered for heavy-duty commercial and executive office use.

- To get more useful help from sales staff, tell them who will use the office and what they'll do in the space. For example, your note "chair for Tom, age 7, and Paul, age 17" translates into "desk chair with adjustable seat height."

- For a fast, easy desk, lay a flat door or wide wood plank atop a pair of two-drawer files. This old college standby

Outfitting Your Home Office

Computers and other electronic equipment change frequently, and software changes constantly. Human beings, thankfully, aren't evolving quite so fast. You'll always need a spacious work surface at the right height, a comfortable work chair, ample storage, and good lighting. Use this punchlist as a starting point when you shop for office furnishings and equipment, but stay open to more convenient upgrades.

- **Accordion file folder, portable file box, or file cabinet.** Two-drawer cabinets are more versatile; they can do double duty as desk pedestals and end tables. They're also less visually dominant. Four- or five-drawer cabinets let you stash a lot more in one compact vertical column, perhaps in a corner.
- **Phone jack and phone with speaker and hold option.** This is essential for multitasking and screening clients from occasionally noisy kids and pets. Add phone service with call-waiting and personal outbound and inbound message recording.
- **Computer with Internet access.** Include virus-protection software, and screening if you have children, plus word processing, financial, photo, and publishing software—or whatever else your business, hobby, and family needs dictate. Many schools expect even young students to have Internet access for homework research.
- **Fax machine** (if you don't fax through your computer).
- **Color laser printer.** This has become a must-have item for a multitude of home and small business projects, including kids' homework.
- **Photocopier** (may be a printer function).
- **Handheld or desktop calculator.**
- **Desk or work surface** for handwriting, project assembly, and holding your computer modem and keyboard if your computer use is light, or a real **computer desk** if you type a lot. It offers a drop-down keyboard tray that holds the keyboard at a healthier angle to prevent carpal tunnel repetitive-stress injuries.
- **Comfortable chair** (casters optional) for light office use, or an ergonomic office chair with casters and adjustable seat height. This is important if kids or other people of various heights will use the desk. Leather is costlier than vinyl but is more comfortable and ages more gracefully. Tightly woven fabric seats in midtone colors hold up better and show wear less than delicate, light fabrics.
- **Hard-surface flooring or low-pile, commercial-grade carpet** plus a clear Plexiglas chair mat or an antistatic mat to protect your computer. All carpet and

almost all hard-surface flooring is subject to visible wear from chair casters, so unless your look is industrial loft style with unpainted cement floors, don't skip the mat.

- **Adequate task and ambient lighting.** You need ambient light from the sun (or natural-spectrum artificial bulbs) to light the room and prevent harsh contrasts. Even more important, you need ample task lighting on every work surface, but not bouncing off of the computer screen.

- **Storage shelves for reference books.** If you tend to throw software boxes and everything else on shelves, plan on more drawers and closed cabinets and fewer open shelves. Don't let visual chaos impede your mood and your productivity.

- **Storage drawers and cabinets.** Choose conventional (deep, narrow) file cabinets, lateral files that look more like conventional credenzas and hold two rows of hanging files, or flat files to stash big blueprints and the like. Choose shallow, wide drawers to hold pencils, rulers, and other supplies without a jumbled pileup. Avoid old-fashioned desk drawers that are too small to hold standard 9×12 file folders; they'll just become the office equivalent of the kitchen junk drawer. Cabinet interiors may be best to stash bulky items, but if it can fit in a drawer, that's easier to access. Remember, if your storage space is hard to get at, you'll be less motivated to keep it orderly.

gives you the basics: ample storage and a generous work surface. A slab of granite or marble, while significantly heavier than a wood door, serves the same purpose and is also more rugged. Seal the stone against stains and you'll have a durable work surface that will last at least as long as your house.

- Invest in the best when it comes to your work chair and your task lighting. You get what you pay for, and you'll pay in discomfort and lost productivity if you try to make do with a poorly made chair and inadequate lighting.

- If you're on a budget, shop used office furniture stores and online for a top-quality office chair. An adjustable-height seat, caster feet for easy movement, an ergonomically formed backrest, and comfortable arms are the

Care of Computers and Other Electronic Equipment

Whether or not your at-home business originally involved much computer use, these days it's almost impossible to avoid being "plugged in"—and, really, there are not many businesses that have become *less* efficient due to technological advances. Keep all electronic equipment running well with careful maintenance and cleaning.

- Protect your computer from serious damage caused by carpet static: Put your computer desk on a hard surface part of the floor or use an antistatic mat.
- Occasionally wipe your computer keyboard with a clean, lint-free wiper. Use an antistatic cleaning fluid now and then, but be sure to spray it on the cloth, not on the keyboard (this goes for all electronic equipment, including screens).
- Make sure air can circulate freely around the computer (and other electronic equipment) to avoid heat buildup that can cause serious damage. Never block the slots in electronics that are designed to let heat escape.
- Always use correctly wired, three-wire electrical outlets for your computer system (and any other home electronics, such as microwave ovens) to safely ground your equipment. These outlets also eliminate electrical "noise" from your refrigerator's motor and other household appliances and minimize interference with TVs and radios.
- When you buy a new computer, check your homeowners policy to be sure you are covered if your computer is stolen or damaged.
- Always back up your computer files onto an external hard drive or CDs and store them safely.

minimum you'll want for long work sessions. If you're shopping online, stick to name brands and check return policies. If you're shopping used office furniture stores, try out the chairs yourself and make sure all the mechanisms work before you buy.

- A drop-down keyboard is important to prevent repetitive-stress injuries to your wrists. If you don't use a conventional desk with a pull-out keyboard tray, choose a table or desk with a lower work surface (about 26 inches from the floor rather than 30 inches).

- When planning the size of your main work surface, figure the area taken up by your computer monitor and key-

board, plus at least 24 inches clear on each side. Set up
your printer just outside this area so you don't have to get
up to retrieve print jobs.

- Add a small desktop shredder to your equipment list to
protect your identity and your privacy, and station a recycling wastebasket beneath or near it.

- Commit to spending ten minutes at the end of each day
to organize your desktop and an hour at the end of each
month to clean up and put away completed project files.

- If your work surface is small, put the computer tower on
the floor out of the way and save space on the desk for the
monitor and keyboard. Make sure you have longer computer cables, however, to make this work.

OFFICE DECOR

- If your office is part of a shared family space, continue the
color scheme and furnishings style for visual continuity.

- If you are lucky enough to have dedicated office space,
furnish it in a way that's as far as possible from the standard office. Pamper yourself with a warmly elegant
executive office or express your creativity with an artistic,
colorful space. If you plan to see clients in your office,
enhance your business credibility with a well-organized
space that reflects your strengths. An interior design business needs a different "vibe" than a computer consultant
or an accountant does. However, the most buttoned-up
job will go better if you are comfortable, and the most
nontraditional one will go better if you're neat and
organized.

- If you are a graphic designer or other creative business-
person, store your best work in plain sight; don't file
it away in closed storage. Use your best, most varied

examples to decorate and accessorize your office. Pro-spective clients will be impressed, and your everyday morale will get a boost too.

- If your office is in the basement, open up your perspective with a painting or poster of an outdoor scene. Those that appear to be looking through a window to the outside are especially effective. Create extra storage by affixing the artwork to a recessed or flush-hung cabinet with dimensions just slightly smaller than the artwork.

- Brighten a basement office, or any small space that's short on windows, with mirrors in window frames. Mirrored storage compartments or closet doors keep storage from visually dominating while expanding your space. The frames don't have to match your existing windows, if any; in fact, this is the place to indulge in a great old salvage window frame as a work of art.

- Give a chic or homey look to your office space by ditching the utilitarian. If you have a treasured mug you don't use because of its gold rim, put it to work as a beautiful pencil cup and enjoy it every day. Instead of ordinary corkboard, cover your bulletin board with a yard of handsome linen or other coarsely woven fabric that won't

show pinholes. Use a decorative metal planter as a waste-basket. Think function, and you'll find numerous items around the house that lend a playful or elegant feeling to work.

- Create a chalkboard or magnetic board for messages on any surface that's convenient with a few coats of chalkboard or magnetic paint. Magnetic paint can be painted over with conventional wall paint and still retain its magnetic properties. Clever magnets in every style are affordable and widely available, so pick a theme and stock up.

- If you use a magnetic board, weed out its contents on a regular basis as you would your desktop. Keep current price lists, maps, or whatever you need quick access to on the board, along with a few favorite photos and inspirational messages. Don't let your magnetic board become layered over with obsolete information like old phone messages or notes.

LIGHTING

- If your office shares space with another room, rely on strategic lighting to de-emphasize the office area after hours. Supplement desk lamps with reading lamps, accent lights, and candles, and put your general recessed or track lighting on dimmers.

- Be aware of light sources in relation to your computer screen. If your screen will reflect light from windows, fit them with shutters or lined draperies. Station reading lamps where the light will fall on your paperwork but not hit your computer screen. Torchiers that bounce light off the ceiling provide good ambient light, but only use them if your ceiling is smooth and in good shape. Recessed lighting is ideal for ambient, all-over lighting. If your budget doesn't allow for recessed fixtures, can lights on tracks offer great flexibility. Choose cans and tracks the color of your ceiling to make them less noticeable.

- If your home office is in the basement, use natural-spectrum light bulbs to mimic sunlight. Even if you don't suffer from seasonal affective disorder (SAD), you'll probably feel better. A bonus: If you're in a creative field, natural-spectrum light will let you see colors more accurately.

TIGHT SPACES

- Define an office area with a decorative screen across a corner of a room. While not ideal, it may be the best space you can find in small apartments.

- Set up an office in a niche under the stairs, on a landing, in a room with a small alcove, or in a dead-end hallway. Use a roll-down window blind or a tall screen to enclose the niche when not in use.

- Convert a wide, shallow guest room closet into an office niche. If it has a sliding door, replace it with a bifold door or simply remove the door and hide the contents with a decorative screen. Be sure you can get adequate task lighting into the niche. To replace the lost closet space, keep a portable wardrobe you can set up when house-guests arrive.

- To make room for a conventional desk in your guest bedroom, replace a double bed with a sofa bed, but make sure you can actually open the bed with the desk in the room. If there's no space for a nightstand, clear off a section of your desktop for guests. Add a small gooseneck desk lamp or a space-saving floor lamp so guests can read in bed.

- Use a slim, traditional writing table where a desk won't fit. Set it at the side or foot of the bed for a comfortable after-hours workspace, or snug it up as a sofa table behind the couch and pull up an occasional chair as needed. Stash office supplies in attractive baskets or boxes on nearby bookshelves or underneath the table.

- Use built-ins wherever possible to stash office supplies, files, etc. Existing bookshelves fitted with matching baskets or bins work fine. If you have closed storage sections, use those to house printers and other equipment and paraphernalia too big for baskets.

KID ZONE

- To protect kids from online threats, experts advise setting up the family computer in a shared space, such as the family room, where you can keep your eye on things.

- Station a color printer where the kids can use it; many schools at all levels expect students to go online for material and print it out in color.

- Give kids ample workspace in their rooms, even if you opt to keep the computer in the family room. Older students especially may want the option of doing non-computer homework in their rooms. They don't need a huge work surface, but make sure it's big enough to stack up books and spread out homework or school projects. A two-drawer file cabinet or a dresser drawer outfitted as a lateral file offers basic storage. If space is really tight, create a desk nook under a raised loftbed.

CHAPTER FIVE

HOW TO GET CONTROL OF YOUR CLUTTER

Before you spend time and money on more storage furniture, elaborate closet systems, or room additions because you "don't have enough space," look at what's really standing in your way. Chances are it's all your stuff—including a huge amount you don't use, don't need, and don't enjoy.

A lot of home projects have to be done all at once, once you get started. Purging clutter, on the other hand, isn't one of them. This is one job that you can do one trash bag or bin at a time, a few hours at a time, over weeks or even months. Every little bit you do will make a big difference in your quality of life. So buy a box of those heavy-duty trash bags and a few lightweight bins, pop in an energizing CD (nothing nostalgic!), and get started.

LESS IS MORE: PURGE BEFORE YOU STORE

The 19th-century Arts & Crafts genius William Morris is credited with saying, "have nothing . . . you do not know to be useful or believe to be beautiful." Look around: How much of your stuff qualifies on either count? We all keep things because they spark good memories of our best times, because something was a great deal, because an item was a gift, and for myriad other reasons that don't really serve us. But are the items useful or beautiful?

If you're a memento collector, there are many ways to keep your memory-making clutter under control. Start with a scrapbook. These can be beautiful works of art in themselves and of interest to friends, grandkids, and others. Photos, matchbook covers, pressed corsages, baby booties, invitations, and much more can be put into a compact form that fits on a bookshelf.

If your memory-sparking item is big, bulky, or breakable, take a photo of it and display the photo as a treasure. Sell or give away the original, or keep a part of it to stand in for the space-hogging whole. A piece snipped from a quilt or gown can serve as a background for small keepsakes you mount on a scrapbook page or in a shadowbox. If an item is intrinsically valuable, such as fine (not just old) antique furniture, you may want to keep it, but don't use this rationale with more than a piece or two. If it's jewelry, you can have it reset; if it's a christening gown, you can have it professionally framed. If it's vintage clothing, you can donate it to the local high school's drama department. You get the idea. So get creative!

Once you've gotten past the sentimental clutter, it gets easier. Set up six bags or bins, and label them **Toss, Donate, Store, Review, Repair,** and **Keep.**

- **Toss:** If it's torn and a mend will show; if it's stained, chipped, or broken in a way that's hard to successfully fix; if pieces are missing or it's dangerous (frayed electric cord, lead paint); if it's obsolete or just plain ugly—toss it! Don't try to donate it. If you'd keep it in another form, make sure you follow through. If you use soft, old cotton T-shirts as cleaning cloths, fine, but don't keep them in T-shirt form. Cut them into usable-size rags and stash with your cleaning supplies—now.

- **Donate:** If an item is still useful to someone but you don't use it or you have duplicates you use more often, donate it to a friend, to a family member, or to charity. Kids' clothes and shoes, warm outerwear, designer

Continued on page 42

How to Keep Clutter in Its Place

Once you've gotten everything and everybody organized, how do you keep things from getting out of hand again? Neatness maintenance is like weight maintenance: It takes a little bit of mindfulness every day. Try these simple tips to make organization a way of life.

- Make sure each room has at least one convenient, roomy place you can quickly stash clutter if you need to pull the place together in a hurry. A hinged trunk/ottoman, a toy chest, a cabinet, or a covered basket will all work easily. Don't leave items in there indefinitely; make a commitment to clear out the stash in a day or two.
- Resolve to keep a few public areas neat, no matter what's going on. At a minimum, keep the front hallway where guests enter, the living room, and the guest bath neat. Try also to keep the surfaces guests will see and touch clean. Keep a cleaning bucket or basket filled with paper towels, spray cleaner, etc., on hand, and keep basic cleaning products under the bathroom sink cabinets (with childproof latches if you have young kids) for last-minute bath spruce-ups.
- Give yourself a psychological boost: Take a few minutes to straighten up key areas of your house, whether or not they're ones guests will see. If you don't always have time to make your bed, plump up your pillows and throw back the coverings to air. Wipe out the bathroom sink and hang towels neatly. Put dirty dishes in the dishwasher, and wipe the table and counter before you go to bed so you start fresh in the morning. Enlist family members into helping with these simple tasks. It's not too much to ask.
- It may be obvious, but have a specific place for everything you'll be picking up from all over the house. Carry a laundry basket or other receptacle with you as you pick up tools, toys, mail, etc., and drop each item in the kids' room or storage area where it belongs. Even if things don't get put back precisely where they go right away, at least they'll be in the general neighborhood where the kids (and you) can find it.
- No matter what, deposit your glasses, keys, cell phone, TV remotes, and other essentials in the same place, every time. Teach kids this important tactic too: You don't want them losing their house key somewhere in the house!
- Recycle your magazines within two months and your newspapers within two days. If you haven't read or clipped that article already, you probably won't. If you can't bring yourself to recycle magazines, find them a home. Kids' maga-

zines can go to schools, better-quality magazines such as *National Geographic* and paperback books can go to senior living facilities, and fashion and beauty magazines can go to your hair salon or health club. Don't make a big deal of it, just drop them off (remove your mailing address first).

- Open your mail over a wastebasket or the recycling bin and dispose of unwanted mailings then and there.
- Store like with like. It makes sense to have a tissue box in each bathroom but not to have four different places to store winter gloves, tape dispensers, and coupons. Don't duplicate storage places if you can help it.
- Kids seem to generate their own weight in paperwork and specialty equipment, and it's hard to find a specific thing as they're running out the door. To solve this common dilemma, designate specific drawers or cupboards for different extracurricular activities. For example, keep Scouting books and camp gear in one cupboard and sporting gear and game schedules in another. When you're hunting for something in a hurry, at least you'll be hunting in a more limited area.
- Even if your space isn't limited, make it a practice to donate or discard an item when you buy a new version of it. If you feel you must keep one extra winter jacket or pasta bowl "just in case"—fine; but somebody could really use that third and fourth old model. Donate or sell it.
- Borrow an idea from the workplace and keep a 9×12-inch inbox and outbox in your home office and another in the kitchen near the door or wherever you'll be likely to see it. Such items as outgoing bills, due library books, and signed permission slips can go into the outbox for family members to take care of.
- If you use plastic grocery bags as small wastebasket liners, keep a few weeks' worth on hand—not a lifetime supply. Same goes for better-quality plastic bags from other stores. Some stores accept their bags back and recycle them.
- Before you buy more storage furniture, pretend you don't have that option and purge the clutter out of the cabinets and drawers you already have.
- Keep a small inconspicuous wastebasket in each room. If it's easy to toss everyday trash, people are more likely to do so. Don't forget to move newspapers, magazines, and other recyclables to the recycling bin eventually.
- Start collecting addresses of charities, facilities, schools, and churches that are looking for books, baby clothes, and other things you have to donate. You'll feel better about letting them go if you know they're going to someone who needs them.

Continued from page 39

clothes, and formal and classic business attire will usually find a home, as will functional items such as furniture and appliances that are a bit outdated but in good condition. You may want to try selling these items on eBay or at a yard sale before donating them, but don't expect to make a killing. These days, with many stores routinely selling new goods at 50 percent off retail prices, you'll probably have to sell at 75 percent off (a $100 item for $25, etc.) unless it's something intrinsically valuable or a really hot collectible.

• **Store:** Off-season items you actually use, such as ski gear and holiday decorations, should be stashed somewhere safe but remote from your everyday closets and cupboards. This follows the basic rule of storage: Keep the most-used things in the most-accessible locations. Once you've purged all the clothes you don't wear, take the pledge to use your coat closets and bedroom closets only for clothes worn regularly, not for clothes you wear only occasionally. Store out-of-season clothes in basement closets or boxes. Store natural-fiber clothing with cedar chips or moth balls to prevent insect damage. Store leather in muslin or another bag that lets the leather "breathe"—never in plastic bags. Store silver in anti-tarnish cloth bags to omit one more chore during the busy holiday season. Whatever you do, clearly label the front of every container to avoid tedious guesswork later.

• **Review:** If you can't bring yourself to unload certain things that you don't use, store them off-premises and date the box. Look at them again in one year, and if you haven't missed them, sell or donate them. Yes, there are exceptions: If you have a soon-to-be independent child and you have an extra blender or chest of drawers, it's smart to keep them. Just don't keep them in your current living space.

- **Repair:** Many things cost more and are not as well-made as their predecessors, so if the item is useful and you can fix a small tear or break, it's probably worth it. If you don't have the skills or time yourself, find a tailor, an electrician, a carpenter, a watch repair shop, a furniture repair expert, or another skilled person to put your things back in working order. Ask friends and neighbors for referrals. (Older people raised in an era when folks repaired rather than tossed things often have great contacts who don't charge an arm and a leg.) Put everything that needs fixing in a bag or box near the back door, and commit to taking it to the repair shop this week. But be honest: If you don't really need it (perhaps because you've already replaced it), sell or give it away to someone who does.

- **Keep:** This is the good stuff—the things you use and love to look at often. They fit you, your space, and your lifestyle. The things you're keeping should be things you use often, but there's one good exception: decorative accessories. If, after going through this process, you still have more accents than you can attractively display at once, divide them into two, three, or four groups, and only keep out one group at a time. Change them seasonally or several times a year, and your eye will appreciate them anew. Plus, fewer items out means fewer items to dust!

ORGANIZING YOUR PHOTOS

If you haven't converted all your old 35mm photos to digital files, you probably have drawers, boxes, and bins full of pictures waiting to be put into albums or scrapbooks "as soon as you get time." Pictures are precious because they carry our memories; in fact, many people say that, after family members and pets, family photos are the first things they'd save in a fire. But if yours aren't organized, you can't really enjoy them, and the next generation won't be able to either. Here's how to get control of your photo collection.

- Collect all of your photos in one place, including the ones still stuck in the processing envelopes from the drugstore and the ones in fancy frames you haven't really looked at in years.

- Get an opaque plastic trash bag for discards (it has to be opaque so you won't second-guess yourself) and some boxes to stash sorted photos in when your project is interrupted.

- Sort your photos into large categories, such as you and your spouse's family, your spouse's family (now and when he or she was growing up), your own family of origin (now and when you were growing up), school pictures, birthday celebrations, vacations, weddings, holidays, friends, other celebrations and milestones, sports photos, etc. Start with large categories; you'll find that subcategories will suggest themselves as you sort photos into piles. For example, a large category like "Vacations" will probably subdivide into "Las Vegas," "Italy," "Disney World," and so on.

- If one objective you have is to create an album for each child, start now. As you sort the "Birthday Celebrations" pile, for example, it's easy enough to subdivide that group into "Jason's Birthdays" and "Michelle's Birthdays." At the end, you'll have a set of photos that include a number of family members, one that largely focuses on one child, and one that largely focuses on another child. Kids of all ages will usually enjoy helping with this project.

- As you sort, throw out photos that are duplicates or near-duplicates, out of focus, overexposed or underexposed, boring, too far away to really see your groom or graduate, or of people and places you don't recognize. Throw them out without thinking twice!

- Unless you only have a few photos of a person, throw out any pictures that are unflattering. It's unfair to remember someone that way. And feel free to toss those unflattering pictures of yourself too. Your kids won't want them either!

- If you have old family photos from several generations back, label them on the back with archival-quality photo labels (available at craft, office supply, and photo specialty retailers as well as online). Write the name, date, and whatever else you want to record on the label before you affix it to the photo.

- When you've gathered all photos of a particular vacation together, label the backs with any specific information you'd like to keep, whether it's "Chartres Cathedral, France" or "Mad Teacup Ride, Disney World."

- Work in one- or two-hour blocks if you tend to get mired down in nostalgia—unless you have a family member willing to help at your side. Then, the sorting exercise can be a rewarding one.

- Send your irreplaceable old photos out to a reputable professional agency to be reprinted and, if necessary, repaired and restored. (You may be able to do it yourself with a photo editing software program.) Display the reprints and store the originals in your safe deposit box or in a fireproof safe.

- Instead of continually buying new frames and adding to your clutter, reuse fine frames. Remove older studio and large school photos from their frames and store them in clear plastic sweater boxes so they'll stay dust-free. Clear boxes work well to store other school photos and sports team photos too. Or store several prior years' worth of large school photos behind the latest one. They'll stay safe and you and your child will enjoy seeing how he or she has grown and changed. Display your latest larger pictures and enjoy them and your favorite frames anew!

• If you know you won't find time to make scrapbooks for most of your photos, store them so you can enjoy them anyway. Buy a batch of attractive photo boxes, label them, and store your sorted 4×6-inch and smaller photos on a bookshelf where friends and family can easily retrieve them. Or buy several large albums with easy-to-use plastic sleeves and stash photos quickly by whatever category you like. (Archival albums are better than plastic sleeves for long-term storage of fragile photos, but sleeves are better than crumpling them up in drawers.)

• As you sort, you'll probably find a number of photos you'll want to display more prominently. You can attractively frame smaller photos in a group with montage mattes that feature two to 16 openings under one frame. Look for a simple, chic design so that attention stays on your photos. Smaller photos demand closer examination, so a multiphoto display like this is perfect for a narrow hallway or another spot where pictures will be seen close-up and at eye level.

• Whether you're using a collection of small, charming frames or one multiphoto montage frame, don't be afraid to crop out unimportant elements to fit your frames. When you trim a photo to remove the area of lawn, carpet, or background that doesn't really help tell a story, you're left with a much more appealing close-up.

Photo Display Ideas

Photos are among the few things you can store and show off at the same time, just by hanging them on the wall. Here are a few decorator's tricks to help you make the most of your photo displays.

• Large, professional studio photos deserve pride of place over the fireplace mantel, over the bed, or on another focal point wall. Photos 9×12 inches or smaller will get lost on a large wall and will look better if massed with other photos. A pair of 9×12s or one 9×12 surrounded by smaller photos will have enough visual mass to stand out. Whatever you do, don't string a series of photos across a long wall, each photo on its own. Group them into pleasing compositions instead, and leave blank wall areas for visual breathing room between groups. (Before pounding nails in the wall, arrange your composition on the floor so you can "eyeball" where to position each picture in relation to the others.)

• Black-and-white photos look best in black or silver frames. For best effect, don't mix color and black-and-white photos in the same display area.

• Professional wedding, school, or other milestone portraits can be grouped to tell a story, either on a wall or on a large piece of furniture. For a cohesive look, use similarly styled frames in the same material and color; for example, traditional silver-finished wood (easier to care for than silver or silverplate frames), modern brass, etc.

• Silver-framed photos on a grand piano are a symbol of glamour, but it's best not to stand anything on such a delicate musical instrument.

- Be careful how you display photos on a table. Make sure the backs are toward the wall. In general, coffee tables or sofa tables aren't the best bet for displaying framed pictures as they expose the backs of frames to some areas of the room.

- If you have lots of small photos on a single theme, such as your dream vacation, have fun with them: Display them under a glass top on a coffee table for a unique conversation piece.

- If you find you and family members don't tend to look at photo albums much, put a few dozen favorite snapshots in a big beautiful bowl on the coffee table or in the front hallway for everyone to enjoy. (Don't do this with fragile heirloom photos, however).

HELPING OLDER FAMILY MEMBERS GET ORGANIZED

It's a challenge to organize one's own things, and even more of a challenge to help children get their acts together. These tasks are easy, however, compared to the delicate process of helping elderly parents or other family members organize their worldly goods in preparation for a move from the family home. Some parents will be mentally able to help direct what happens to their possessions but may not have the stamina to take care of the job themselves. Others may be less able but may still have strong sentimental attachments to their belongings. Here are a few tips to make the process a little easier.

- Whether your parents are moving from the family home to a condo, a senior-living or assisted-living facility, or a

Designer Tips for Uncluttered Display

Fewer, larger, better-quality decorative accessories are the style in the new millennium. But many people still love to collect. If this is you, create a cleaner, more sophisticated look and cut down on your housework at the same time. Rotate accessories seasonally, and if you still have a lot of small items to display, don't strew them all over every surface. Instead, set them up in odd-numbered groups of three to nine pieces. Group according to theme, color, item type, or some other aspect they have in common. Create one or two of these tablescapes, and leave other surfaces clean to provide visual relief (and less dusting). Better yet, store all your small items in a glass-front cabinet for an impressive display and less clutter throughout the room.

Use the same concept to organize wall art. While you want to spread large pieces of furniture and large wall art evenly around a room for a balanced look, you'll want to group, or mass, small accessories and artworks. Instead of strewing small pictures on all four walls, group them together, an inch or less apart, in a composition that pleases you. It makes a more dramatic, less cluttered impression and gives you fewer areas to dust.

nursing home will affect how many belongings they can bring. If the situation is uncertain, it may be best to put many of the furnishings in remote storage. If the situation is more stable, find out exactly how much space will be available in the new dwelling, both for furnishings in use and for personal storage space.

• Help your parents identify the major furniture pieces they will take with them. In general, the best of the smaller, more versatile pieces will serve them better than large, bulky ones. For a move to a small apartment, a drop-leaf dining table or one with leaves removed may work fine, for example. Large sectionals, sofas, king-size beds, wall units, and trestle-style dining tables that can't be broken down may be difficult to accommodate. Fortunately, these are seldom the pieces with great sentimental value.

- No matter what their new living situation, don't overlook the importance of your parents having at least a few of their favorite furnishings and pieces of artwork around them. There is some indication that these familiar touch points help elderly people retain their bearings longer, and it almost certainly will help their adjustment and their morale.

- To get it right the first time, draw a to-scale floor plan of the new residence, and measure furniture items to be sure they'll be placed in a workable location. This process can reassure your parents that things are under control and proceeding according to plan.

- Help your parents identify the furniture, artwork, and other items of real and sentimental value they want to take with them. They may be willing to apportion off other items to grown children, or they may opt to sell or donate their things to a favorite charity. Don't rush this process: Plan to take a week or more to help them select and divide their belongings. If possible, segregate items that will be given away or sold in a guest room or another area so parents won't have to second-guess themselves.

- Help parents notify all heirs who may have an interest in the belongings that won't be going with them. If parents can make specific gifts to individual heirs themselves, that's ideal; if not, you may have to ask heirs what specific items are meaningful to them. In a perfect world, every heir will choose different items and there will be no hard feelings. In reality, you may need to use a system other families have found fair: Heirs each take turns choosing one item until everything has been dispersed. (This method can also be used to distribute belongings when parents are no longer in the picture.)

- Use the same multibag system (see pages 39–43) you used for organizing your own home to help parents toss, donate, store, and keep small items. Attics and basements are often filled with things parents haven't seen, or missed, for decades. When it comes to bigger items that are still functional but not worth selling, contact a charity or simply put them out by the curb. Small salvage operators cruise many neighborhoods in the early morning and will pick up virtually everything that looks usable, so you can avoid the pickup fee charged by some cities.

- When sorting and packing, don't overlook the shoeboxes, bookcases, and other hiding places many people use to stash money and other valuables. If parents are able to take part in this process, a simple reminder may be enough. If not, you'll have to help them carefully go through things.

- Pack everything with care in small, manageable boxes and label them clearly to avoid stress at the other end of the line.

- When it comes to housewares, if your parents will be in an apartment, they'll still need cookware but perhaps not every small appliance, gadget, and dish. The same applies to tools, hobby materials, and other items beyond basic clothing and health-care items. Help them choose their most used, most versatile favorites and apportion out the rest. Again, store the giveaways out of sight once the decision has been made.

- If the home is to be sold, once your parents have identified pieces they want to take with them, ask the real estate agent what pieces, if any, should be left in place to help sell the house. These can be given to family members or sold after the house sells.

- If you can't be there to help with this process or if emotional issues are becoming a problem, consider bringing in a helper who is not a family member. A friend or a church group or club member who is closer to the parents' age may be a comfortable choice. If this is not an option, contact a social service agency near your parents' home for a referral.

- While boxes of canceled checks don't need to make the move, elderly parents do need certain important paperwork. These include a current will, the name of the executor (usually the family lawyer or one of the adult children) who holds the second copy of the will, and the location of military discharge papers, insurance policies, bank accounts, and safe deposit keys. Some parents will indicate that they will be organ donors and have written end-of-life directives and their memorial preferences. (If your parents don't bring it up, you might approach the subject by saying you won't need the information for a long time but you'd feel better having it out of the way.)

- Keep in mind that parents' most important legacy is the family itself. Don't let "stuff" come between family members. After all, they are the ones who will carry on the parents' best-loved traditions and memories.

CHAPTER SIX

ORGANIZING CLOSETS

Closets deserve their own section in any organizing plan because so much of our "stuff" ends up there—along with the clothing we need to access daily. Get your closets organized, and your whole home will be easier to keep neat.

MAXIMIZING CLOSET STORAGE

The outside perimeter of your closet may be fixed, but all the interior dimensions can change to fit what you need to store in it. Whether you're adding a new closet, putting a closet system into an existing closet, or just reorganizing the closet using dividers you buy at the store, always start with a clear, well-thought-out plan (yours or yours and a professional's).

Whatever your closet size or plan, make sure you include a full-length mirror (on the outside of the door or on a wall with an unobstructed walkway of at least four feet so you can approach the mirror) and lots of good lighting inside the closet. Today's new compact fluorescent bulbs yield a pleasant light and last longer and aren't as hot as incandescent bulbs. Depending on the size of the closet, one good light fixture overhead or a series of lights, recessed or on tracks, will let you see what you've got. Install ceiling fixture lights in the middle of the closet ceiling or far enough out in the space so that the light falls on the clothes and is not obscured by shelving. Avoid halogen or other hot lights in closets; hot lights, flammable materials, and tight spaces make for a bad combination.

- A closet remodeling is like any other room redo: You'll need to accurately measure all dimensions of your closet and draw an accurate replica of the space. Inches count!

- Assess your wardrobe and other items you'll want to store in your closet to see how much space you'll need for each type of item. If you wear suits occasionally but cashmere or silk sweaters daily, you'll need more space to safely store folded, delicate knits than you will hanging jackets. Group all your like items together, such as all blouses in one section and all slacks in another, and measure how much space each section takes, vertically and horizontally.

- To avoid crowding clothes on the closet rod, allow one inch of horizontal space per garment; allow two to three inches of horizontal space for each suit, sport coat, and jacket, depending on the bulk of the shoulder padding. Based on these allocations, you can easily figure out how much space you need for each category of clothing. For example, 12 skirts would occupy 12 inches of horizontal space, and three suits would occupy six to nine inches of horizontal space.

- To figure vertical space, measure the lengths of your garments from the top of the closet rod to the bottom hem of the garment itself. If most of your skirts are 20 inches long but one is 22 and two are 21 inches, use the 22-inch length. If you have one or two items that are quite a bit longer—for example, one 28-inch tea-length skirt amid all the 20- to 22-inch skirts—set up your closet for the 22-inch length and hang the odd longer item with your long evening skirts.

- When figuring vertical space, consider the style of hangers you use. Hangers with short necks may position a garment three inches closer to the rod than those with long necks to give your closet more vertical space.

- Don't want to bother measuring your own stuff? Use this quick take: Hang a single rod somewhere between 63 and 72 inches above the floor. If you're using shoe racks below, make sure the rod is high enough to keep long gowns or robes from dragging on the racks. For double rods, hang the upper one between 76 and 84 inches above the floor and the lower one 36 to 42 inches from the floor.

- Assign your clothes and accessories to specific locations inside your closet. Determine what should be hung on hangers, hung from hooks, or stored on shelves or in baskets. Allot everything rod space, shelf space, floor space, or space on a specialty rack.

- Install your clothing rods at least one foot from the back of the closet to avoid crushing garments. Allow at least a three-inch minimum clearance for rods hung under shelves so you can remove hangers freely.

- If your closet has a conventional door, install hooks, shallow shelves, or hanging bins to transform the inside of closet doors into useful storage areas.

- Plan to keep a six- to eight-inch section of your clothing rod empty of everyday wear and use it for dry cleaning, both incoming and outgoing.

- Men's shoes take up more room than women's, and men's jackets are bulkier than women's, so don't assume a particular storage piece works equally well for each. Measure a few typical items, such as athletic shoes and suit jackets, to be sure closet compartments can accommodate your size.

- A do-it-yourself closet job with stock components works best when your closet isn't an odd, one-of-a-kind layout.

A closet with a sloped or lower than normal ceiling; with masonry, plaster, or brick walls rather than wallboard; or with windows, vents, or other unusual structural components inside the closet may restrict the materials you can use. The shape and size of your closet may also limit the location and installation of any organizing materials you buy. In these cases, consider bringing in a professional.

- If there's enough access to interior closet wall space, plan for grids on the sides of closets to store belts, bags, and scarves that take up little space but lots of shelf room.

- If you have obstacles inside your closet—air ducts, a water heater, etc.—plan to store objects there that fit the space. For example, if you have a narrow space between the closet wall and an air duct, fit it with shelves and store items like bags and shoes.

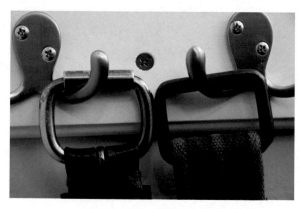

- Use the inside of the closet door for belt racks and hooks that hold necklaces or other nonbulky items appropriate for hanging. (Laundry bags are not appropriate here, for instance. Any type of storage rack that is bulky or protruding will get in the way and push up against the clothes inside the closet.

- Take advantage of cubbyholes, which work well for keeping stacks of sweaters conveniently contained and categorized, or for keeping handbags and purses in an upright position for easy access. This method allows you to clearly see each item without digging through various layers. It also opens up shelf space inside the closet.

SAMPLE CLOSET CONFIGURATIONS

Standard Wall Closet (42 inches wide)

In general, because of the door's position, you'll want to install a shoe rack on the left side wall. This shoe-storage method requires only five inches of space to operate efficiently. Install racks for ties, belts, and scarves on the opposite side wall at the same heights as closet shelving to ensure enough vertical space for the lengths of the belts. Divide the height and length of the shelf into smaller compartments by using purse and sweater cubbyholes or other shelf dividers. Use add-on hangers to nearly double the average number of garments the closet can hold.

Large Closet (100 inches wide)

In this size closet, you can incorporate an extra six feet of shelf space, in addition to the full-length top shelf, by adding cubbyholes in a vertical alignment. What's more, this requires giving up only 12 inches of hanging space for extra shelf space. A ventilated system (see pages 61–63) allows the lower shelf and rod to stand free. With a modular system (see pages 60–61), a supporting wall would be needed.

Large Closet (106 inches wide)

This closet is only a few inches wider but there is a major difference—the wall that holds the closet door also offers additional wall space. This provides 24 inches of additional space on each side of the closet for shoe racks or belt/tie racks without any reduction in visibility or accessibility.

Walk-in Closet (size varies)

Walk-in closets offer so much increased wall space that it is seldom necessary to conserve space to the same degree as in a standard wall closet. The main advantage of a walk-in closet over a standard wall closet is not just its increased size but also the opportunity to keep each closet function separate from the others. One entire wall can be used for hanging, another for shelving, while a standard wall closet must combine hanging and shelving on the same wall.

Use the same planning factors for a spacious walk-in closet as you would for a large closet, except draw more than one wall for a complete design. It's essential to understand how each piece comes together in the corners of the closet.

- When the rods and shelves of two walls butt into each other in the corner, that corner space can be functional in only one direction.

- The shorter "inset" walls or the inside surface of the doors supply the perfect spot for belt/tie racks or wall shoe racks.

- A closet with a door that opens inward and is flush with the side wall prevents use of part of the wall for any major closet component. Instead, mirrors can be installed on both the wall and the inside of the door.

Quick Tricks for Your Closet

If you aren't up for a full-scale, professional closet redesign, you can still make big improvements in how much, and how neatly, you store things. Just use these simple techniques.

- Add a second shelf above the existing one to store less-used, bulky items.
- Install an over-the-door shoe organizer that holds 18 to 21 pairs of shoes on the inside of a closet door. You can see what you've got and use less space than storing shoes in their boxes.
- Install two rows of coat hooks on your closet doors—one down low and another higher up. Use the higher ones for your coats and let children use the lower ones. Or hang purses, backpacks, etc., on the lower hooks.
- Install that workroom favorite—a pegboard—inside a closet or cabinet door instead of on the wall to hang small items such as belts, necklaces, and lightweight purses. Be sure to leave space behind the pegboard panels for the hooks.
- Not into do-it-yourself projects? Just use sturdy boxes stacked on their sides (or set a narrow bookcase on its side) to compartmentalize your shelf space. Things stay neat instead of jumbled in piles, and you can store less-used items on top of the boxes.
- Once you've purged your closet of things you know you won't wear, hang your clothes by category: skirts, suits, slacks, blouses or shirts, and dresses and gowns or long robes. Then, within each category, hang pieces by color. This will make your closet look more professional and make it much easier to see what you have and put together outfits. It will also help you keep from buying yet another black sleeveless top or blue-striped dress shirt.

HOW TO CHOOSE A CLOSET SYSTEM

If your budget allows, hire a professional closet company to design and install your new closet system. If you have more time than money, do the analysis yourself and assemble the pieces from your local storage specialty shop. Either way, your new closet system will most likely be one of the following types. Pick the one that best fits your circumstances and your needs.

Separate Shelf/Separate Rod System

This traditional style of closet is typically seen in older homes where the closet hasn't already been renovated. The shelf or shelves are usually wood, and the closet rod is wood or metal. The shelf is supported on each side wall and along the back wall by strips of wood that are nailed to wall studs. The shelf itself isn't permanently attached; it can be lifted off the wood strips and removed from the closet. The rod is either separate from or fused with the hardware, which is attached to strips of wood installed on the side walls. When these wood strips are removed, holes are left in the wall.

Advantages: Since no extra features such as racks for shoes, ties, or belts are built in, you have the freedom to place them where you want them.

Disadvantages: At least a small degree of carpentry skill is required, and your modern closet system must be installed between two supporting walls.

Costs: The cost of this system depends almost entirely on the quality of the wood you use. This system is usually comparably priced to a ventilated system (see opposite page) and costs approximately a third to a quarter less than even the least expensive prepackaged modular system. Designing, purchasing, and installing the components yourself will cut the cost by almost half.

Modular System

This is a separate shelf/separate rod system with an upscale appearance. Modular systems consist of presized cubicles and shelves with structural dividers, giving more definition to the closet space. The structural dividers let you create compartments to keep your belongings to a specific area in your closet with either a wood or metal rod. Sometimes, a plastic-coated metal rod is offered in a range of decorative colors.

Advantages: Modular systems may be modified or custom designed to fit the size of your closet and what you want to store there. Some offer a wide variety of features that make them very adaptable.

Disadvantages: The structural dividers eat into your closet's space, reducing the actual space you have available for storing your belongings. This isn't a problem when you have a closet of reasonable size and dimensions, but it can be critical in a smaller closet where every inch counts. Also, preconstructed (noncustom) modular systems offer a limited number of sizes and shapes, so you can't always place or hang things exactly as you'd like. It's especially hard to accommodate a modular system to closets that are particularly small or oddly shaped.

Costs: The quality of the materials used in construction as well as the number of features you choose greatly affect the price, which can range from affordable to expensive. Cost is also affected by the amount of planning and figuring work you are willing or able to give to the project. The more you can do yourself on the project, the more you can save.

Ventilated Closet Systems

A relatively new type of closet design, ventilated closet systems are constructed from metal rods covered with a vinyl or epoxy chip-resistant coating. The diameter of the rod inside the coating is the most important factor to consider:

The smaller it is, the less sturdy and dependable the system will be. Carefully investigate the hardware used for installing these systems to make sure it's reliable. Purchase only a system with attached wall anchors; don't buy one that has unsheathed screws. Precise measurements are a must, and a little know-how in handling a drill is helpful.

Advantages: Ventilated systems save space because the overhanging front edge actually becomes the closet rod, extending a mere two inches below the shelf itself. All other closet systems require at least four to six inches for the same service. Ventilated systems can solve the problems presented by unusual wall configurations that otherwise would just be wasted space. For example, they allow the corner area of your closet to hold hanging clothes, something no other system can do. There is also a track system option that lets you easily adjust the heights of the shelves.

Disadvantages: Ventilated systems have vertical struts built into the front edge every 12 inches for added stability. These struts don't allow you to slide a hanger the full length of the clothing rod. However, if your closet is properly organized, there should be no reason to push the hangers aside. Ventilated systems need support braces every 12 to 24 inches, and these also keep you from sliding your hangers the length of the rod. Look for newer redesigned versions with the brace secured at the top of the shelf, leaving the rod area clear.

Costs: The cost of a ventilated system is comparable to that of the separate shelf/separate rod system (see page 60).

Prepackaged Ventilated System Kits

These kits come in a box containing the necessary pieces to assemble a ventilated system yourself.

Advantages: If you find a kit that fits your specific needs, it's certainly less trouble to carry home just one box. Kits include instructions to guide you through the installation process.

Disadvantages: For any given closet, there are a limited number of possible configurations, restricting the number of possible designs. You might see an unassembled kit designed precisely as you would like your own finished closet to be, but that kit may not be suitable for your closet's size and shape. You may get lucky, but it's more likely you'll have to do some compromising.

Costs: Unless they're on sale, prepackaged kits seldom cost any less than buying the components separately. In fact, kits can cost a little more because you're paying for precut lengths.

CHOOSING CLOTHES HANGERS

Something as simple as clothes hangers have a lot to do with how well your closet does its job. Note these tips for maximum efficiency (and minimal aggravation).

• Don't use plain wire hangers. They tangle because their necks are too small and narrow, they can damage your clothing, clothing straps always fall off of them, and they always fall off the clothing rod. If you accumulate a few from the dry cleaners, recycle them or drop them back off to the cleaner, who will be glad to reuse them.

• Plastic tubular hangers are easily available and inexpensive. Many of these hangers include notches, but thin shoulder straps or the hanging loops inside the waistband of a skirt may slip out. If you must use these hangers, choose ones with small plastic hooks instead of notches to hold straps securely. Plastic tubular hangers come in a variety of colors; encourage kids to hang up clothes by stocking their closets with hangers in their favorite hues. You may also find clear plastic hangers with bigger notches and a heftier profile; these can work for menswear and even coats.

- For most efficient use of space, choose metal attachable (also called add-on) hangers with multiple skirt/trouser clamps that let you hang two, four, or more items from one hanger on the rod. These hangers have an extra hook in the center that allows another hanger to be attached to the hanger above. Add-on hangers let you hang clothes vertically as well as horizontally across the closet rod, so you can get a lot more clothes in the same horizontal space. If you don't need additional hanging space, use attachable hangers to open up space for shelves, cubbyholes, drawer units, or other storage devices inside your closet.

- For pants, use a hanger with a tubular horizontal bar to keep pants from getting a horizontal crease. Better yet, use open-end slacks hangers. These have a movable bar that allows slacks to slide on and off the open end of the hanger but snap into a small bend to hold securely when you want it to. The neck is bigger and rounder than most other hanger types, so it won't get tangled with other hangers on the rod. Slacks hangers are also shorter in length and width than most hangers, opening up areas of the closet where a standard-size hanger cannot go.

- Business suits and winter coats are heavy, so use a coat hanger with a substantial, contoured frame of wood or sturdy plastic designed to keep the shoulders of these garments in place. Coat hangers with a horizontal open-end slack hanger feature are perfect for suits. You can also find coat hangers with clamps for skirt suits. Coat and suit hangers are typically wider and bulkier than other hangers, so be sure your closet is deep enough for the number of suits and coats you need to store. If you have a separate coat closet near your front door, store bulky winter coats there and save bedroom closets for suits. Keep a half dozen extra of the contoured wooden coat hangers in your coat closet for guests; it makes a luxurious impression.

• Protect delicate silk blouses and dresses with fabric-padded hangers. The fabric may be charming printed cotton or a silky poly-satin or microsuede; some even have scented sachets inside. Experiment to see if fabric-padded hangers will hold spaghetti-strap tops; the cotton and microsuede ones often will (satin is sometimes too slippery). Fabric-padded hangers are a thoughtful touch for guest rooms, but they're often smaller than average so may not work for men's clothing. Add a few nice wood hangers and you're covered.

HOW TO STORE FOLDED CLOTHES AND SMALL ACCESSORIES

Whether you store sweaters, stockings, and other folded garments in compartments within your closet or, more commonly, in dresser drawers, use these tips to keep things neat and easy to find.

• Divide larger drawers or closet compartments into smaller, more manageable ones that more closely match the size and shape of the items they hold. Keep like with like: sweaters, knit sleeveless shells, etc.

• Use acrylic shelf dividers to segregate a whole shelf into specifically assigned storage compartments. These dividers are perfect for handbags, sweaters, hats, and more.

- Use drawer organizers to arrange articles in a drawer so that each article is plainly visible. Drawer organizers make socks, stockings, underwear, rolled ties, and other small items easy to find.

- Roll sweaters rather than folding them. Place the rolled edge up and align the sweaters in the drawer single file from front to back or side to side so that each sweater is visible and handy.

- Keep belts neat and out of the drawer with a belt rack that you install on the side wall of your closet.

- Protect expensive neckties and make them easy to select on busy mornings with a tie rack. Choose a model that you install on a closet wall and that lets you see all your ties by extending the rack's arms outward. The arms fold back into the unit and the unit slides back into its original position. An alternative is to fit small acrylic tie storage units into a dresser drawer and roll each tie to fit. You'll be able to see them all at a glance.

- Store jewelry so that it's safe from damage and tangles. If possible, choose a unit that will let you easily see all your options. Jewelry boxes let you store items of various sizes and, if you don't have a lot of jewelry, should work well for you. Be realistic about how much jewelry you have (and actually wear); a standing, multidrawer jewelry chest on legs may be what you need.

- Individual bags and pouches protect jewelry but make it harder to see what you have. Sterling-silver jewelry may be stored in antitarnish bags, but pearls are delicate and shouldn't be in contact with any chemically infused material. (This includes faux pearls, as many are made of genuine mother-of-pearl coatings over plastic.) Eighteen- or 24-karat gold is softer than 14 karat and is easier to bend or scratch; sterling silver is also relatively soft. Precious metals should be stored in felt-lined drawers to prevent damage.

- If you're the accessories type and have lots of costume jewelry necklaces, hang them from hooks where they'll stay tangle-free and you can see them easily. Expandable cup holders or multiple garment hooks designed for front halls can be used to hang costume jewelry necklaces as well.

- Fine silk scarves are easily snagged and wrinkled; protect your investment with compartment inserts for drawers, but buy good ones: You need to be sure they have no burrs (rough edges) anywhere. Roll scarves as you would ties so they stay wrinkle-free. Inexpensive scarves can be hung from hooks; set up a hanging accessory area with hooks for necklaces and scarves nearby.

- If you have an estimate from a professional organizing company, compare it with the cost of doing it yourself. Nearly every product and accessory is available to the everyday consumer. If you have basic carpentry skills, doing it yourself will reduce labor costs, but be sure to include the cost of any tools or special equipment required and the value of your time.

- Remember that when existing storage structures are removed, holes, scratches, and other unsightly conditions will be left behind. It demands less time and less energy if the closet or storage area is patched, prepped, and repainted before the new system is installed. Don't forget to include this extra expenditure in the total budget for the project.

CHAPTER SEVEN

HOW TO GET ORGANIZED ALL AROUND THE HOUSE

Do you find it impossible to grab a rake from the garage without having five garden tools come barreling toward you? Do you often struggle to find a spice for tonight's dinner without rummaging through the ten spices you *don't* need and never use? And let's not even mention those winter gloves and mittens that mysteriously lose their mates each year. If these sound like some of the dilemmas you routinely face in your home, it's time to make getting organized—all around the house—a priority. Let's begin with organization tips for everyday living before moving on to specific areas in the house.

- Add shelves above or near your washer and dryer to hold colored plastic baskets, one color for each family member. When you take clean clothes out of the dryer, sort each person's clothes into the appropriate basket. Family members can then pick up their baskets and fold and put away their own clothes.

- Keep two large bags near your dryer. As you notice items that need mending or items that should be discarded, you can simply store them in your "mending" bag or "give-away" bag until you're ready to deal with them.

- For the family room or any place you have more stuff than space, consider making or buying a storage ottoman. If you're handy, build a simple toy chest or hope chest–style piece with a hinged, flat top. Make sure it's at a comfortable seat height, and add a cushion for additional seating. Also use safety hinges (ask at your hardware store) to keep the lid from slamming down on fingers.

- Being neat doesn't come naturally to most kids, but clutter makes life stressful for them too. Help them by setting up colorful cubby compartments, bins, baskets, and hampers at their level. Most clothes today are wrinkle-resistant, so even if they don't bother to fold their clothes, at least they'll end up in the generally right spots. Pick your battles: Separating clean from dirty and tops from bottoms is a good start.

- Use clothespins to clip gloves, boots, and gym shoes together so family members don't have to rummage for pairs. Use plastic sock clips, available at home organization or hardware stores, to keep pairs together in the wash.

- Use hanging fabric shoe holders for other items as well. Store small plush collectible toys, knitting and other craft supplies, small tools, and more in these handy compartments that keep things off the floor but in plain view.

MAXIMIZING EXISTING STORAGE SPACE

Ready-made shelves can be installed just about anywhere to create storage for books and decorative items, toys, glassware, china, and anything that will fit on a 6- or 12-inch ledge. If you intend to store heavy items, make extra sure the brackets are securely anchored. Here are tips for using every bit of storage space possible in places you might least expect it.

- Use a wide hallway for extra storage; line the wall or walls with a shallow, tall bookcase or a shelving/cabinet combination.

- Built-in bookcases around and above a door make a handsome, upscale-looking storage solution. If your budget doesn't cover this kind of project, use freestanding book-cases as tall as the door opening to flank the doorway, and install a narrow bookcase sideways above the door, flush with the sides of the flanking cases. Paint all the cases white or the color of your walls for an elegant built-in look and lots of storage.

• Can't clean the whole place at once? To screen the mess of a small walk-in closet or pantry, slide a twin-size sheet onto a spring-loaded curtain rod and hang it in the doorway.

• If your home has an enclosed staircase, it's hiding valuable storage space. Work with a carpenter to see if yours can be opened up to create space for closets, niches, shelving, or even a small desk. Your understair storage can stash little-used and seasonal items behind a cabinet door, or store books or toys on open shelves.

• Replace conventional nailed-in-place steps with hinged steps. Use the space under the hinged steps to hold boots or sports equipment.

MAXIMIZING GARAGE STORAGE

Today's garage is likely to house excess belongings of all kinds, as well as cars. In fact, some are so filled with holiday decorations, bikes, large toys, sporting equipment, garden tools, and home accents, there's hardly room for vehicles. Fortunately, since you don't have to be concerned with decorating conventions in the garage, you can look at every square foot of wall space as potential storage. Follow these tips to get your garage back.

• If your budget allows, use a storage specialty company to design the ideal system for your garage. **Remember:** The system will only work if you account for all of the belong-ings you want to store there and tell the company agent what items you use often, seldom, etc.

- Hang as many items as possible on the walls to maximize floor space. Bikes, sleds, and many other equipment items can be hung with ropes on nails or hooks; or you can buy specialized bike racks to install on the wall. Rakes, bats, brooms, and other cylindrical items can be pushed between spring-loaded clamps you nail to the wall at appropriate heights.

- If you have a workroom area in your garage, keep small items out of the way but visible. For example, store nails and screws in glass baby food jars.

- Use the top portion of walls to store little-used items; you can always use a stool to reach them. Install shelves or cabinets on the top half of your garage's back wall, but make sure you install them high enough so that the hood of a large car can easily clear the shelves. (Your current car may have a lower profile, but you'll want your storage plan to be flexible for future vehicles.)

- Use a garbage can to store long-handled yard tools, and attach hooks to the outside of the can for hanging up smaller tools. You can lift up the whole can and move it to whichever part of the yard you're working in. Better yet, you won't have to deal with putting tools away individually at the end of an outdoor workday when you're likely to be tired.

- Install a platform across the garage ceiling joints to create a large storage place for infrequently used items.

How to Organize Your Car

Do you know somebody whose house is usually neat but whose car looks like a dumping ground? With today's commutes getting longer and longer, it's easy for car "housekeeping" to get out of hand. Follow these tips to take control again.

- Make it a rule to take out everything that doesn't belong in the car every night, especially food wrappers, bank deposit slips, and anything else you'll wish you had removed. Insist that the kids remove their trash and belongings too.

- Set a good example for the kids by clearing out the not-so-decorative distractions you've accumulated, such as stickers, view-obstructing novelties hanging off the rearview mirror, obsolete maps, parking stubs, and other items you've stuffed behind the sun visor.

- Don't leave electronics, your briefcase or purse, or anything else that poses an obvious temptation in plain sight in your car. Take it with you or lock it in the trunk (but take the keys with you).

- Even if you belong to a motor club, be sure you have a complete emergency kit in each car you own. The kit should include safety flares, flashlights, chains, working jumper cables, blankets, a water bottle, and a first-aid kit, at a minimum. Roll tools in an extra old blanket to keep them from clunking together.

- Keep your car insurance card, a copy of your registration, your motor club card, any warranties or guarantees for replacement of tires or other on-the-road service you're entitled to, the car's owners manual, a tire gauge, a pen, a notepad, sunglasses, a small flashlight and extra batteries, some pain reliever, often-used maps, and other important items in the glove compartment.

- If you have kids and they eat on the road, keep a box of disposable wipes and a roll of paper towels in the car and pass them out before the in-car dining begins.

- Set up a small plastic trash bag on the passenger-side floor in front so you can dispose of rubbish immediately.

If you're traveling with kids or others in the back seat, furnish a trash bag for those passengers too. Remind kids that it's not the eating in the car that makes the smell and mess, it's leaving food and wrappers in the car.

• Keep kids entertained with a mesh bag of small toys, books, and electronic games that hooks over the front seat and hangs so kids in the back seat can reach it. Choose toys that have numerous moving parts that are all attached rather than those with small loose pieces. A multicompartment cup holder that sits between kids (use the safety belt to keep it secure) can help corral small writing tools and toys as well as keep drinks and snacks from spilling.

IMPROVING KITCHEN STORAGE

Mountains of books and magazine articles have been written about kitchen design, many focusing on the storage function. Check them out to gather ideas, but don't be swayed by the endless advertising for the latest organizing products and gadgets. Decide what you need for the space you're organizing, and then search for the product or materials that will do the job.

Whether you're building a new kitchen, remodeling your existing kitchen, or just looking for ways to improve what you've got, you can extract more useful storage space out of the hardest working room in the house.

• Save time and steps with an efficient work triangle. The total distance from sink to range to refrigerator should be at least 12 feet but not more than 22 feet. Work areas should be no closer than four feet nor farther than nine feet from one another. Shorter distances mean you are too cramped; longer ones mean you must take tiring extra steps. If you're not remodeling, consider moving the refrigerator or the range if your kitchen is extremely inefficient.

- Go through your kitchen cupboards and drawers and get rid of items that you don't use. Throw out junk, donate anything that might be useful to someone else, and store things that you rarely use elsewhere, such as in the attic or basement.

- Go through the "junk" drawer. Chances are you'll find something that you're ready to throw out. Add a drawer divider from the office supply store to keep pens, small notepads, carryout menus, and the like under control.

- The most convenient storage is between shoulder and hip height, which is why so much stuff ends up parked semipermanently on the kitchen counter. If you have room in your kitchen or in an adjacent space for a pantry, you can store most-used items on shelves between shoulder and hip height without hogging prep-counter space.

- Some appliances will end up staying on the counter. Be sure they're the toaster and coffeemaker you use once a day, not the bread machine and fondue set you use once a year.

- Hanging the microwave above the range is passé and inefficient. Unless you're the only cook in the house, hang your microwave below a cabinet, not above the cooktop. You want to be able to use your range for serious cooking while another family member heats something in the microwave. If you have younger kids, don't hang the microwave at all. It's too dangerous for them to lift out hot foods and liquids above their shoulder level. Set the microwave on the counter instead.

- Why is it important not to let clutter and unused appliances hog your countertops? You need to keep at least 18 inches and preferably 24 inches of countertop on at least one side (and preferably both sides) of the cooktop, oven, refrigerator, and microwave clear at all times to land hot, heavy, slippery, and breakable items in a hurry!

- Whether you use pantry shelves or kitchen cabinets, for safety's sake, always store heavier items at waist height or lower, and store lightweight, small items you can lift with one hand on higher shelves.

- If you can choose between cabinets with pullout trays or drawers, choose drawers. Drawers eliminate the second step of having to open the cabinet and then pull out the tray. However, if you're not remodeling your kitchen, do install pullout trays in fixed lower cabinets. They're much better than cabinets you have to reach into.

- The corner cabinet where two walls meet can be a great waste of space or offer great storage. Install a lazy Susan turntable in lower cabinets (or a cabinet with the turntable built in, if you're remodeling). You can store bulky blenders, bags of dog food, big colanders, and more.

- Install a shallow, wide cabinet or pull-out pantry on the open end of a run of front-facing cabinets or drawers to hold cans and small boxes of food. If you're not doing a whole remodeling, create a similar effect with a shallow, wide bookcase unit. You can store a lot of packaged foods without taking up much more of the kitchen floor space.

- If you're remodeling with semi-custom cabinets and have a narrow space left over, install a narrow (four-inch) slot the height and depth of a base cabinet to hold baking sheets. Simpler yet, just lean baking sheets along one interior sidewall of the sink cabinet.

- Stemmed wine and water glasses can be stored upside down with the help of special gripper inserts that hold the stems. You can stash short glasses on the shelf below this setup if the area above the shelf is tall enough. Don't try it if the dimension is close; you don't want to bang crystal into everyday glassware.

- Flatware trays are easy to find, but measure your silverware drawer before shopping. You may be able to fit two trays in one drawer if you buy the smallest-scale tray that holds your silver. Use the other tray to organize all the small items (corncob picks? cocktail forks? baby flatware?) that end up floating around otherwise.

- When storing means stacking, protect delicate dishes and nonstick cooking pan surfaces by always layering a sheet of paper toweling between stacked items.

- Storing cups and other dishes on open shelves looks cottage-charming, but unless you're a microwave- and carryout-only kind of cook, you'll have to wash them before you use them, every time. What works in open storage? Big decorative trays, antique china pitchers, fancy tureens, and other attractive but seldom-used items.

- Store dinnerware near the dishwasher so it can be emptied quickly or near the table so that it can be set easily.

Storing Food Safely

- Always check the label on boxed and canned food items to see how they should be stored. If you have not refrigerated items that should be, throw them out.
- Hot air doesn't do foods any good, so use cupboards or open shelves above your cooktop for nonfood items only.
- Don't store foods under the sink where they could be damaged by sweating pipes or in cupboards that contain cleaning supplies.
- Certain foods, such as bananas, potatoes, and onions, should not be refrigerated but should be kept cooler than most foods stored in cupboards. In the absence of Grandma's old-fashioned root cellar, store these foods in mesh bags in the coolest place possible. Apples may be refrigerated but don't need to be; keep them cool and they'll last for several months.
- To prevent dangerous bacteria growth, always refrigerate or freeze fish, poultry, meat, milk, and other dairy products immediately after you buy them, and never thaw these foods and then refreeze them. Fish, shellfish, poultry, and ground meats are especially fragile and prone to spoilage even if refrigerated, so cook as soon as possible if you're not going to freeze them. Don't let blood or other liquids from raw meat, poultry, or fish get on wood cutting boards or any other porous surfaces, and be sure to immediately clean granite or other hard, nonporous countertops immediately with an antibacterial cleaner or bleach.
- Freeze foods in odorless, moisture-proof, airtight containers such as rigid plastic or glass containers with tight-sealing lids, zip-top plastic freezer bags, and heavy-duty plastic film or aluminum foil.
- To avoid spoilage and explosions, store home-canned goods out of direct sunlight and direct heat sources.
- Do as they do when stocking grocery store shelves: Store newly bought foods behind those already on your shelves to be sure you use the older ones first.

- Many people cook daily but bake only weekly, if that often. A separate cooktop and oven lets you add more everyday storage below the cooktop. Install your oven on a wall outside the work triangle.

- Don't install a cooktop, an oven, or a range next to the refrigerator. It is inefficient design and makes the fridge work harder than it has to.

- Cooktops set into islands are popular but not safe if you have young children. Instead, put the main sink or a second prep sink in the island and keep the hot spot on an outside wall, out of reach and out of everyday kitchen traffic.

- If you have more floor space than you need but less storage space, install a peninsula or an island in your kitchen. An island can provide a convenient landing spot/prep station if the distance between sink, range, and fridge is too long for efficiency. Islands on wheels are available in many styles and can be taken out of the room entirely if need be. An island only 18 inches wide can hold 12- or 18-inch cabinets underneath. To install a sink in the island, the cabinet should be at least 36 inches wide.

- Set small turntables in eye-level upper cabinets to easily access twice the items without unloading the cupboard. Double-tray turntables are great for storing twice the spice jars in a small space.

- Install a flat knife rack inside a high cabinet for hanging sharp knives to save drawer space and keep knives out of children's reach. If you don't have young kids, use a knife block and place it in a corner where two counters meet.

- To economize on drawer space, arrange wooden spoons and other utensils bouquet-style in a handsome pitcher, canister, or wooden bucket near the range or on the counter.

MAKING THE BEST OF BATHROOM STORAGE

The bathroom is typically the smallest room in the house yet has so many necessities busting out of its drawers and cabinets. Make the best use of this small space by getting toiletries, towels, and other bathroom accessories in order.

- Before you start organizing, conduct a thorough cleaning of existing bath storage. Get rid of outdated or unflattering makeup, old personal care items and medicine, frayed or grungy-looking washcloths and towels—all the clutter that collects in the bath.

- Invest in an over-the-toilet storage unit. They're available in a variety of attractive furniture styles. Be sure to pick a unit that includes some closed storage as well as shelving.

- Hang wicker baskets on the bathroom wall for storing hand towels, bath toys, and other incidentals you don't mind being seen. But don't let them become the equivalent of a junk drawer at eye level.

- Color code cups and toothbrushes. Have each family member choose a different color to prevent confusion over belongings.

- Install a row of towel and robe hooks behind the bathroom door, or use an over-the-door unit that just slips on the door.

- Hang shelves or small closed cabinets in the "dead" wall space beside the vanity, over the toilet, or behind the door.

- If you're remodeling the bath and you have a little extra room, choose a narrower sink cabinet and install a three-drawer unit next to it. Drawer storage is easier to access than cabinet storage, and the compartments help enforce neatness. Look for one shallow drawer and two deep ones to hold hair dryers and other bulky items.

- Put a small plastic basket or two inside the top drawer of the bath cabinet (or in the medicine cabinet if you have small kids) to corral nail files, clippers, scissors, and other small metal objects.

- Hang a shelf-and-hook storage device over the shower-head to stash small shampoos, razors, washcloths, and more. These ventilated shelves let water drain and reduce mildew by allowing air around items. Do clean the wall and suction cups with bleach a couple of times a year.

BOOSTING BEDROOM STORAGE

- Bedroom storage is not limited to clothes, shoes, and jewelry. Make use of any unused space for storing extra sheets and blankets, favorite books, decorative treasures, and the like.

- If you have upper wall space, buy or build a headboard storage unit. Set books, lamps, a clock/radio, etc., on top of the unit and other items inside.

- For a double-duty ottoman, set a sturdy, flattop blanket chest at the foot of the bed to stash bulky comforters and extra pillows. Top it with a cushion and create an extra spot to sit too. Or, if you're handy, build a plywood box with a hinged cover. Paint the outside or cover it with fabric, and add the seating cushion.

- Buy two letter-size, two-drawer file cabinets in an attractive wood style to match your décor, and use them as nightstands flanking your bed. You'll gain roomy storage and keep important papers close at hand.

- If you're buying a new bed, look for one with under-bed drawer storage, sometimes called a captain's bed. The look is handsome, and the storage is unbeatable. Or buy roomy, shallow rollout bins for under-the-bed storage. They can hold bed linens, craft or sewing supplies, extra table leaves, infrequently used clothing, and virtually anything flat and oversized for normal storage.

- Use hooks or an accordion cup rack on the wall to hang attractive hats, jewelry, and scarves.